The Berenstain Bears'®
SHOW-and-TELL

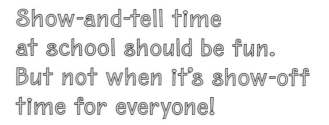

Show-and-tell time
at school should be fun.
But not when it's show-off
time for everyone!

Mike Berenstain

Based on the characters created by
Stan and Jan Berenstain

HARPER FESTIVAL
An Imprint of HarperCollinsPublishers

HarperCollins
PUBLISHERS
Since 1817

Sister Bear used to enjoy show-and-tell at school. It was supposed to be a time when cubs could bring in their special things from home and share them with their classmates.

Show-and-Tell

But lately she felt that show-and-tell time was becoming show-off time. Everyone just seemed to bring in the newest, shiniest, most-complicated, and most-expensive gizmos and gadgets.

It all started when Millie Bruno brought in a brand-
new cell phone her parents gave her for her birthday.
All the other cubs wanted one, too. They marched right
home and begged their parents for cell phones.

Some parents gave in—but some didn't. The cubs who didn't get one were pretty grumpy about it. This included Sister since Mama and Papa thought she was still too young for a cell phone.

Another show-and-tell was coming up soon. Sister decided to bring in her favorite Bearbie doll. That seemed safe. But before it was her turn, her friend Lizzy Bruin stood up.

"This is my brand-new Fit-and-Trim Super-Exercise Bearbie," said Lizzy proudly. "She's the latest thing— she can do jumping jacks, crunches, push-ups, and knee bends. I used to play with a regular Bearbie doll. But this one is even better!"

When it was Sister's turn, she hid her old Bearbie behind her back and mumbled that she had forgotten to bring anything. At the end of the day, Brother joined Sister as she gloomily trudged her way home.

"What's the matter?" he asked. "Did someone rain on your parade?"

"Someone poured cold water on my Bearbie," she replied, and told her tale of show-and-tell woe.

"Hmm!" said Brother, thinking it over. "Maybe you should try something really different for show-and-tell and stay away from toys and gadgets and things like that."

"But what else is special enough for show-and-tell?" asked Sister.

They found a gold statue of a bear holding a
water vase. She had a clock in her tummy.
"What about this?" asked Sister.
Brother shook his head.

"Too silly," he said.

"What about this?" asked Sister.

She put on an old moth-eaten Great Bear War uniform. It hung down to her feet. Brother shook his head.

"It smells funny, and it's way too big for you," he said.

"Wait a minute," said Sister. "What's this?"
Behind one of the boxes, she found a big green hoop.
"Wow!" said Brother. "That's an old Twirl-a-Hoop.
Let's give it a try."

"This is how you use it," explained Brother, holding it around his middle. He tried to twirl it, but he couldn't seem to get the knack. It just fell down around his ankles.

"Let me try," said Sister. She turned out to be a Twirl-a-Hoop wiz. "This is terrific!" she said, Twirl-a-Hooping up a storm.

"This will be perfect for show-and-tell," said Brother. "You can give a Twirl-a-Hoop demo. You'll start a new fad!"

And so, at the next show-and-tell, Sister brought in the old Twirl-a-Hoop from the attic. No one except Teacher Jane had ever seen one before. Sister twirled and twirled.

The class loved it—they clapped and cheered. Of course, everyone wanted a turn. But Sister was the best. That is, until Teacher Jane took a shot at it.

"I haven't tried one of these in years," she said. "But I used to be pretty good at it. Well, here goes!"

Teacher Jane *was* pretty good at it. In fact, she was great! She was even better than Sister.

"Go, Teacher Jane, go!" yelled the class.

They made so much noise
that Principal Honeycomb
came to the class.

"What on earth?" he began sternly. But then
he saw the Twirl-a-Hoop. "A Twirl-a-Hoop!"
he said. "I haven't seen one of those in years.
Here, let me have a try!"

As Principal Honeycomb twirled away, Sister realized something important. Things don't necessarily need to be brand-new, complicated, or expensive to be special. Sometimes the plain and the simple—or the old and the forgotten—can be very special, indeed. And that's well worth showing-and-telling about!

"Lots of things," said Brother. "Old family treasures can be very special. What about all the stuff up in our attic?"

"Oh yeah!" said Sister. "I didn't think of that."

When they arrived home, they gave
Mama, Papa, and Honey quick hugs,
then eagerly climbed the stairs to the
attic. It was a little dark and spooky up
there. Boxes were piled on top of other
boxes; strange shapes were leaning
against other strange shapes. But there
certainly was a lot of interesting stuff.

The cubs began to look through the boxes piled on boxes. They found all sorts of unusual things.